Benares

OrangeBooks Publication

1st Floor, Rajhans Arcade, Mall Road, Kohka, Bhilai, Chhattisgarh 490020

Website: **www.orangebooks.in**

© Copyright, 2024, Author

All rights reserved. No part of this book may be reproduced, stored in a retrieval system, or transmitted, in any form by any means, electronic, mechanical, magnetic, optical, chemical, manual, photocopying, recording or otherwise, without the prior written consent of its writer.

First Edition, 2024
ISBN: 978-93-6554-485-5

BENARES
Where Myth Comes Alive

KRISHNA

OrangeBooks Publication
www.orangebooks.in

तत्पुरुषाय ॐ विद्महे महादेवाय धीमहि तन्नो रुद्रः प्रचोदयात :

Om Tat Purushaya Vidmahe Mahadevaya Dhimahi
Tanno Rudra Prachodayat

"I bow to Lord Shiva!"

Acknowledgement

As the final page turns and the last word lingers in the air, I find myself filled with gratitude for the that brought this story to life. To my journey family, your unwavering belief in my dreams has been my anchor. Thank you for your patience during countless hours of writing, rewriting, and pondering the fate of characters who often felt more real than the world around me. Your love fuels my imagination.

To my friends, particularly my fellow writers and readers, your insights and encouragement helped refine this tale. You provided the much-needed laughter, coffee, and late-night brainstorming sessions that turned ideas into adventures. Thank you for being my sounding board, my critics, and my greatest supporters.

A special thank you to my editor, whose keen eye and thoughtful suggestions have polished this manuscript into the shimmering gem I hope you hold in your hands. Your belief in the story made all the difference.

To the realms of inspiration: myths, legends, and the histories that weave our world together. Thank you for whispering secrets into my ears and gifting me the courage to explore the unfamiliar.

Lastly, to the readers—thank you for embarking on this journey with me. Your curiosity, passion, and willingness to dive into a world of fantasy make the entire endeavour worthwhile. I hope my words transport you, challenge you, and ignite your own sense of wonder.

May your own adventures be as rich and enchanting as the one found within these pages.

With deepest gratitude, Krishna

वक्रतुण्ड महाकाय सूर्य कोटी समप्रभा।
निर्विघ्नं कुरु मे देव सर्व-कार्येषु सर्वदा॥

BENARES!!!

Normally when someone hears this, they think about the Oldest surviving city in the World. But those who have visited, will tell you it's more, much more than that. For a moment if you can silence the crowd and other noises, you will find you transcended to a surreal world, which swings between ancient and modern. The architecture around takes you back ancient times, whereas a youngster sitting on the steps playing on his Mobile brings you back to the modern era.

Without further ado, let me take you through a story which will question what is real and what is fiction as it is aptly said "Truth is stranger than Fiction". The story will take you through the rarely taken streets of time and old age ancient wisdom of few Golden age people who still are able to read the ripples in time and space consortium when you ask them about the ancient truths, which while sustaining the Sands of Time have slowly changes from Truth to Myth.

The story is seen from the eyes of a Human, whose close brush with history which he thought to be myth or bedtime stories from old people, makes him grasp his wits when he comes face to face with them during which he thought to be a casual visit. Sometimes, you have to shed the spectacles of Modern times to be able to see through the mists of time and know the truth of our ancient ones. The stories will question your understanding about ancient Banaras. You thought you know enough of its history. But, in reality ***DO YOU?***

ॐ त्र्यम्बकं यजामहे सुगन्धिं पुष्टिवर्धनम्

उर्वारुकमिव बन्धनान्मृत्योर्मुक्षीय माऽमृतात् ॥

Table of Contents

Pratham Adhyāya
Morning Aarti 1

Dwitiya Adhyāya
Shamshaan Ghat 10

Tritiya Adhyāya
Assi Ghat 17

Chaturtha Adhyāya
Forgotten Legend 29

Pancham Adhyāya
From Myth to Reality 35

Shat Adhyāya
Ashwatthama 41

Saptam Adhyāya
Ancient History 47

Ashta Adhyāya
Monster from the Abyss 53

Nava Adhyāya
　　The Quest 61

Dasha Adhyāya
　　Purification 69

Ekaadasha Adhyāya
　　The Fight 77

Antim
　　A New Beginning 90

Pratham Adhyāya
Morning Aarti

Krishna, woke up at 3 AM with a start hearing the shrill sound of the Mobile Alarm. While, staying on the bed with his eyes open, his life scrolled behind his eyes like a movie. A Cyber security professional who has been busy building a successful career all his life, in order to give his family all the luxury which he missed during his childhood and youngster days. Coming from a poor family, he knows the daily struggle for money. After 36 years of commitment and hard work, now he was able to break free from the 9-6 corporate cycle and visit one of his best Friend from childhood – Mahadev's place of worship, BANARAS. Reaching, yesterday evening, he was unable to explore the city and had set the alarm to watch the world-renowned morning Aarti at Assi Ghat.

Realizing time slipping away as sand, which it usually does when you are lost in pleasant memories, he jumped from his bed shedding the sleepiness in an instant. Getting ready as soon as he can, and only taking with mobile with him he started towards the Assi Ghat with a spring in his steps, due to the anticipation of the Divine Aarti darshan. It's like a dream come true for him and also, he wanted to approach some of the Sadhus and Aghoris to hear some of the old stories he was intrigued since childhood about this Divine Abode of Mahadev and also how much truth they hold. There was still some way to go when the divine sound of Conch and Ghantas arising from the Ghat put a hurriedness in his steps as Aarti was about to start. Stepping on the Assi Ghat Road from Nagwa Road, he was treated to a view so Divine that, he couldn't decide whether to Cry or Laugh. He could only bow hie head with folded hands, tears streaming from his eyes and a smile on his lips.

He took a few minutes to grasp himself and moved like in a trance towards the Divine event happening before him. The Aarti at Assi Ghat in Banaras. According to legend, Maa Durga threw her Khadag into the Assi River after killing the Rakshasas Shumbha-Nishumbha, creating the ghat. This act symbolizes the victory of good over evil. Assi Ghat is located at the confluence of the Ganga and Assi rivers. The lights which were still on shown like a path of light from the Asisangameshwar Lingam, adding mystery to the Misty morning. It seemed came out of a divine trance once the Aarti was over, with hairs across his hands standing at its end. He stood up with the sounds still echoing in his ears, minds and banks of Assi Ghat to explore the Ghats. His eyes were taking in the beauty of the Ghats, parallelly searching for someone to clear the mist covering his mind. There were crowds of Sadhus, Saints, Aghoris, however he was unable to connect with any one of them. After roaming around for almost one hour, with hunched shoulders he sat down on the steps staring at lights on the other end of the fast-flowing river, loosing himself in thoughts.

While shitting at the banks Krishna, was watching loads of tourists who were hiring boats to go downstream towards Chet Singh Ghat, Dashashwamedh Ghat, Kashi Vishwanath Temple, and other Ghats of Divine city Banaras. After roaming here and there, and getting a plate of Chat from a shop he sat down listening to the tinkling sounds of Kashi Viswanath temple. **Kashi Vishwanath Temple** dedicated to Mahadev. Located in

Vishwanath Gali, is one of the twelve Jyotirlinga shrines. The Lord is called by devotees by the names Vishwanath and Vishweshwara, which means Lord of the Universe. It is the first Jyotirlinga to manifest itself. According to the ancient history, it was at this place that Mahadev manifested as an infinite column of Jyotirlinga in front of Brahma and Vishnu when they had an argument about their supremacy. In order to discover the origin of the luminous column, Vishnu took the form of a boar and tracked the column beneath the ground, while Brahma, who assumed the shape of a swan, scoured the heavens in an attempt to locate the apex of the column. However, both of them were unsuccessful in identifying the source of the luminous column. Yet, Brahma deceitfully asserted that he had discovered the summit of the column, while Vishnu humbly admitted his inability to find the starting point of the radiant column. Due to Brahma's deceit over the discovery of the origin of the luminous column, Mahadev penalised him by cutting his fifth head and placing a curse upon him. This curse entailed that Brahma would no longer receive reverence, whereas Vishnu, being truthful, would be equally venerated alongside Shiva and have dedicated temples for eternity.

There are twelve self-manifested jyotirlinga sites that take the name of the presiding deity; each is considered a different manifestation of Mahadev. At all these sites, the primary image is a lingam representing the beginningless and endless Stambha pillar, symbolising the infinite nature of Shiva. The twelve jyotirlingas located across Bharath are Somnath, Mallikarjuna,

Mahakaleswar, Omkareshwar, Kedarnath, Bhimashankar, Viswanath, Triambakeshwar, Baidyanath, Nageswar, Rameshwar and Grishneshwar. However, no other place had that pull for him as this place.

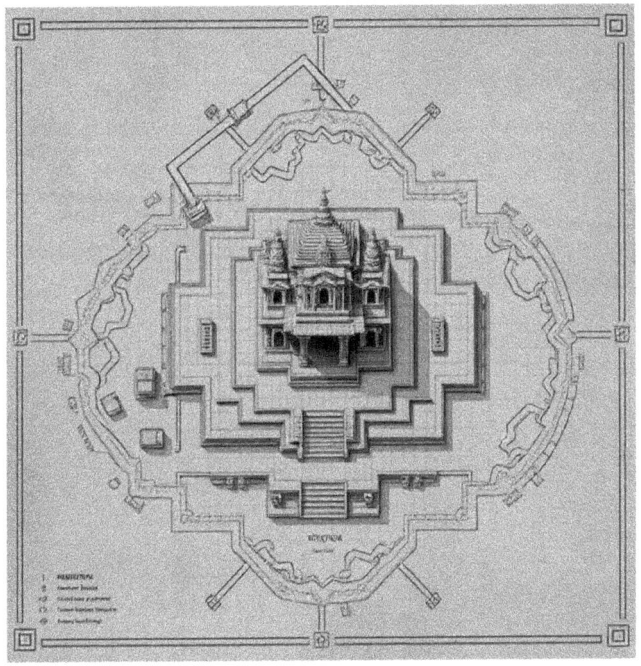

Plan of the Ancient Temple of Vishveshwar.

Suddenly he remembered an old quote by **Mark Twain**: *"Banaras is older than tradition, older even than legend and twice as old as both of them put together."* Listening to chants by a group of tourists 'Kadam to rakho Kashi mein, tar jaoge Kashi mein.' Legend has that the funeral pyres at the cremation grounds of Manikarnika and Harishchandra Ghat never cool down. It is the only place in the world where Life and Death come together in harmony and co-exist. Another famous place Kashi Mumukshu Bhawan is a hostel which caters to the needs of the dying. Between all these thoughts fogging is mind a voice of "Chai Chai" comes tearing the mist, waking him up from his memory slumber. He extended ten rupees note to the hawker in return for a Kulad of Chai in this wintery morning. Grasping it with both hands appreciating the warmth his mind went back to his original thoughts as to why this place had a special pull for him since childhood. The Pashupatinath Temple bells ringing in tandem took him back to the time when he was a 6-year-old kid sitting on his Dadi's lap hearing the Story of Maa Durga and Shumbha-Nishumbha. As a six-year kid also he had the same question he has today – "Where is the Khadag which Maa Durga threw and why nobody tried to find it?" The answer given by his Dadi had imprinted itself in his soul. "The Khadag waits to be discovered by someone worthy during the times of grave danger, when evil raises it again".

Just like any human, Krishna's mind also went in to an hypothetical imaginary world. With all the wars and terrorist attacks across the Globe the rise of evil seems imminent and to stop that, how if found he can use the Khadag. Just like a kid with a new toy, he kept creating different scenarios in his mind and the use of the Khadag for the situations, in all those deriving a serene pleasure in making some difference, although in an imaginary world. Suddenly, he jumped out of his skin realizing a hand on his shoulder. He was so deep in his thoughts that he never realized it is past morning and the crowd has swelled as the river flowing in front of him. Looking up, he was staring up at a serenely calm face with greying dreads flowing from his head and face. With nothing but a single loincloth on his body, the Aghori had ash all across his body with a mystic smile and a spark in his eyes, hiding something mysterious. As if reading Krishna's line of thoughts and questions he uttered a single word "Come". Like an obedient pupil, Krishna followed him to a boat tied near the Ghat. The boatsman who looked in his early sixty's wearing nothing but a T-shirt and a dhoti in this chilly morning smoking a bidi sat there expecting rides. His sunken eyes lit up watching two people approaching him, expecting his first income of the day. The Aghori approached him and informed the destination. Krishna could see a shadow of fear passed over his face hearing the name but only for a fleeting moment. He welcomed them on his humble boat and made them as comfortable as he can. Pushing his boat in to the swirling waters he starting humming some long forgotten local tune while paddling them towards their destination. His co-passenger, the Aghori still had that mysterious smile on lips while looking in to the distance which amused Krishna a little. He was still unable to grasp why he believed him so unconditionally without an iota of suspicion.

There was a torrent of questions in his mind at the Ghats, but now there was a calm which looked like the calm before the storm. They were travelling smoothly over the mighty Ganges whose waters have cleaned up a lot after the Namo Ganges project taken up by the Government of India. Krishna was again lost in thoughts looking at the flow of water under their boat. Where exactly was the Khadag thrown? He had gone through hundreds of books by both national and international writers. Visited numerous libraries, spoke and consulted with many Dharm gurus, Katha Pravachaks, sadhus, saints, Tantriks, etc to know the exact place where the event occurred. However, alas none were able to give him a satisfactory or even close answer to his question. That is when he had fallen back to technology which was his strong point. The swirling waters below started a Kaleidoscope of memories in his mind of his journey. To quench his thirst for answers, he had started studying sacred texts, Pandulipis, Tad patras travelling across Bharath and speaking to many sages to get to know the exact date and time or visual description of the event. After almost getting disappointed that all his efforts are in vain, he had accidentally stumbled upon a saint in his hometown near the not so well known Ramchandi Temple on the Puri Konark Marine drive road. Krishna had driven from Puri towards Konark on the Marine drive road which had always calmed his nerves with the serene beauty and sound of waves of Bay of Bengal, crashing on the shores. He had stopped near the temple to enjoy the beauty of the sea when he noticed a modest saint taking rest below a tree.

Krishna couldn't understand why he had a sudden urge to walk up to him. Throwing the butt of the cigarette down, he went ahead and before he could decide whether to wake him up or not, he opened his eyes with a smile on his lips. He sat down and motioned Krishna to sit beside him. Like an obedient child he walked up to him and took a seat. Without any small talk he asked a few questions about Krishna's life and then asked what he wants to know. Krishna asked him the same question which he had asked a thousand times to many people and to himself as well during all those sleepless events between mugs of coffee. "Guruji after Nidhaan of Shumbha-Nishumbha when did Maa Durga throw her Khadag in to the Assi river?" There was a mysterious smile on the Sage's face and he narrated the same event which led to the demise of Shumbha-Nishumbha. Then Maa arrived at Assi Ghat to throw his Khadag in the river. Then he went on to explain the position of planets during the event of Shumbha-Nishumbha demise and after what duration Mata arrived at Assi ghat. Krishna's eyes lit up with the information. He pulled up his Laptop Yoga from his backpack and opened the Star Chart software to know the exact date and time by entering the position of planets and particular stars at respective positions. His eyes lit up with the information shown on the screen. That is when he made up his mind to visit the long-awaited Banaras and more specifically Assi Ghat.

Dwitiya Adhyāya
Shamshaan Ghat

A sudden splash of water on his face from the waves hitting against the boat broke his chain of memories and dragged him to present. The boat was plying upstream creating major ripples in the water. Here and there a flower garland, or a small kalash, or a piece of cloth floated by raising a few questions in Krishna's mind. With a sudden jerk of the boat touching the land, he got pulled out again from his chain of thoughts. The letters shown on an old name plate at the bank sent a chill running through his spine. The rusted board read "**Shamashaan Ghat - Ramnagar**".

The Aghori got down without a word and stood a few feet away with his back towards the boat. Krishna shrugged his soldiers and pulled out a five hundred rupee note to pay the boatman, who replied humbly that he doesn't have change. Krishna asked him to keep the change and as felt guilty not keeping enough change. While leaving the boat the Boatman caught hold of his hand and whispered "Beta, don't stay until sunset. Get out from here before Dusk" and handed him a piece of paper with a landline number. He whispered again, "Beta call me if you need me anytime, or in case you stay after Dusk as no Boatman will row you out after Nightfall from this Ghat". Leaving a bewildered Krishna on the bank we left. Krishna, put the paper inside his Mobile cover and turned towards the Aghori to ask something. But before he could utter a word, the Aghori raised his hand to silence him and motioned him to follow him. They walked Northwards towards a temple seen at horizon. As they closed near the temple, he was able to read the name "**Maa Kali Aghor Ashram**".

However, the Aghori moved ahead the temple and took a left turn towards the bank.

There were a few funeral pyres burning with less crowd as not many people know this place and even those who know are afraid with all the stories surrounding the place. The Aghori walked towards a thatched hut nearby and after having a glass of water from the earthen pot and offered a glass of water to Krishna. He suddenly realized how thirsty he is as from morning he had only a cup of Chai and it was around 10 AM in the morning. He motioned him to follow him in to the one room hut. There was nothing inside it except a few earthen utensils and an earthen stove with stacks of wood tied up in bundles on one side. The Aghori sat on the bare ground and Krishna followed him. The Aghori started speaking "I know the turmoil inside you, ask freely what you want but beware that the truth is not always to the liking and may be a lot more than you can chew up". Krishna had a moment of hesitation grasping the words, but the thirst of knowledge soon overpowered it. Without wasting any moment, he asked the same question he had asked his Dadi, "Where is the Khadag which Maa Durga threw and why nobody tried to find it?" The Aghori sighed which showed that he had come across this question many times before.

But before he could start, Krishna spoke up once again. "I know the date and time when Mata ji had thrown the Khadag and an approximate place where she may have stood. Can you help me with further information?" Like a candle lit up by a matchstick, the eyes of Aghori lit up and a smile spread across his lips. He understood,

Krishna is not just an average tourist or those new generations who carry mobile phones on a stick who just want some spicy stories. Here was someone who is in pursuit of the truth. For a moment he remembered something he heard from a very old Aghori when he was in trance in the Maa Kali Temple. He was just starting his Aghori Vidya and barely a teenager back then, but those words are still etched in his mind after decades. The Aghori shrugged it off and further asked – "Have you read any sacred texts?". To which Krishna named a few which he had read during his pursuit for the Khadag. The Aghori further asked "What do he know about Kaliyuga and what are his views on it?". To that Krishna answered what he had read in Kalki Purana and how the evil is stronger and manifests itself strongly in this era. To which the Aghori said more than to himself than to Krishna –

"In Satya Yuga Good and Evil existed in different worlds.

In Tritya Yuga Good and Evil existed in same world, but different families.

In Dwapara Yuga Good and Evil existed in the same family.

In Kali Yuga Good and Evil exists in a same person."

The words although were said in a hushed tone, but reverberated like ripples in time. Coming back to the discussion the Aghori asked a few more details to gauze the depth of Krishna's understanding of Kali Yuga. Then he asked "Why do you need to find the Khadag and what will you use it for?". Krishna never thought what he will use for as it was just a treasure hunt before that and had never delved on the practical usage of it. So, he tactically twisted his answer saying – "In case of any evil arises against whom our modern weapons which may seems devastating, do pale in comparison to the ancient Divine Astras mentioned in sacred texts, then such a powerful weapon may be used to save humanity". The Aghori had a mysterious smile on his lips, like a mother would have when he knows her children are lying to her. He again asked – "Which mythological monster you think will some again in Kali Yuga that such a powerful weapon will be necessary?". Krishna was left speechless to it as he understood the Aghori has seen through him. While he was pondering for a way out, he was saved by a old wrinkled face peering inside the hut. The old man, who was the Caretaker of the Shmashaan queried with a parched voice – "Prabhu lunch is ready, kindly come and have it". Krishna looked at his watch and realized it was past 1 PM and suddenly felt very hungry as he had only a plate of Chat after the Aarti. Both of them walked out of the hut and proceeded behind the old man to have lunch.

The old man's thatched house was a bit bigger from the one room hut they were in with a few accessories, like a cot, an old rusted table fan and some steel utensils and a Gas stove with the picture of some Political Leader on it. All three sat down to have a simple meal of Rice, Drumstick curry and a spoon of pickle. The old man took out a small plastic Jar of Ghee and taking a spoonful smeared it on top of the rice on Aghori's plate. To which the Aghori motioned to do the same on Krishna's plate too. Krishna saw that after doing so, the old man ignored his plate and put the jar back. He felt humbled with gratitude seeing this simple act of Atithi Satkaar by someone so poor. The meal tasted better than any Luxurious restaurants he has been during his Convocations, meetings or dinners. After, having a good meal, all three sat on the banks taking in the serene view of the mighty Ganges. The old man was free as during the afternoon rarely any one comes for cremation. They chit chatted some more about the history of Banaras and the famous temples in and around it for some time. The Sun after its daily journey was nearing the end of the Horizon, given a beautiful golden look to the Ganga waters. The bells have started ringing in preparation of Sandhya Aarti. Krishna suddenly remembered the warnings of the boatman. Unable to suppress his curiosity he asked the old man about why people are afraid after night fall. The old man said only one word **"Masan"**, glancing towards the Aghori.

For a moment Krishna thought he is saying Shamashaan, and it also justified why people are afraid to visit this bank where funeral pyres are lit almost continuously. But looking at the Aghori and his fallen gaze a doubt crept, did he hear it correctly? But before he could, the Aghori looked up and staring across the Ganges told Krishna, "It's my fault entirely as I was young and naïve. Anyways, it's getting late, you should go back to Assi Ghat. If you want to continue our discussion, you will find me here after Morning Aarti". Saying this, he walked away towards the small hut. Krishna, realizing he can't pursue it any more, took out the piece of paper which the boatman had given him. Just below the number his name was written **"Drauni"**. I dialled the number and after getting Drauni on call asked him to pick him up from the banks. After around 20 minutes he could see the boat approaching the banks.

Tritiya Adhyāya
Assi Ghat

While boat approached, he noticed something peculiar about the boatman which he had failed to notice before as he was engrossed in his own thoughts. The old man was of impressive height which you would fail to guess when he sat inside the boat. He was surprisingly muscular for someone his age which Krishna thought would be due to rowing the boat all day long. But there was something tingling like an itch at the back of his mind which he was unable to put his finger on. He shrugged his shoulders as he had enough on his mind and didn't want to over exert himself. The ride back was as silent as the morning ride. When Krishna got down at Assi Ghat, it was already crowding up with anticipation of the evening Aarti. When he opened his wallet to pay Drauni, the old man raised his hand and told the five hundred rupees he gave in morning more than enough covered his ride.

Krishna, went to the nearest shop to get a pack of Cigarettes, in order to get loose change for his five hundred rupees note. He got a Kulhad of masala chai and started on a small walk a little further from the Ghat, not to cause any inconvenience to anyone while he smokes. His eyes were stuck on the Pandits who were getting the massive Diyas ready for the evening Aarti. The preparation of the Aarti was at the level of grandeur apt for the King of Banaras – Deva adi Dev Mahadev. Krishna watched the Aarti with the same reverence and awe a toddler has when he sees his father performing some trick to amuse him. After the Aarti, he decided to explore the gullies of Banaras and taste some saviours from road side stalls for which Banaras had a big fanbase between foodies. While coming in the morning he had noticed a shop at the merging point of Nagwa and Assi road. As it was close by, he walked up to there to try some Kachoris. His mouth started watering seeing the delicious foods in the showcase.

After gulping down Kachori Sabzi, Tamatar Chat, washing down it with a glass of Sweet lassi and completing with an assortment of sweets till hi heart's content, he felt satisfied. His hotel was just within 1 km from there, so he decided to have a walk after such a heavy meal in order not to cause indigestion. His one of a kind Rado watch showed its Quarter to nine. Probably a 15 mins leisurely walk. He lit a cigarette and started towards his hotel. He threw the cigarette butt under the soul of his boot and just before entering the hotel he got a fleeting glance of a shadow which quickly disappeared in the nearby ally. May be a casual pass by or any late goers hurrying back to their house. Krishna got freshened up once he reached his room. The hotel housekeeping had done an exemplary work cleaning the room and keeping fresh towels, bedsheets and covers. Krishna took up a book for bedtime reading before going to sleep. Before he could complete the first paragraph he was under a deep slumber.

Krishna again got up at 3 AM when his Mobile alarm started chiming. He was still tired from previous day's experience and thought of snoozing the alarm and sleep into the morning. However, just before his hand touched the snooze button, the face of the Aghori flashed for a moment before his eyes. In that instant all his senses became active and he woke up just as suddenly as he dozed off yesterday night. He went and opened the window to have smoke before getting freshen up. He thought he saw a familiar shadow again disappearing in to the nearby ally. Not dwelling further on it, he quickly freshened up and started towards the Assi Ghat. All along he had a feeling he was followed or, was it paranoia since he saw the shadow or something else. The experience of Assi Ghat was exhilarating as his first visit. After watching the Aarti he had a light breakfast with a Kulhad of Chai. His eyes were searching for Drauni with whom he somehow felt a bond. Drauni, was sitting on the bow of his boat arranging the ropes of his boat. Krishna approached him and said hi with a smile on his face. Drauni, smiled back at him and as if by mutual understanding they both boarded the boat and started to yesterday's destination.

When he reached the bank the Aghori was waiting for him as if in expectation. Krishna got down and gave the fare with some tip money which Drauni, politely returned back. Just like the day before they walked in silence towards the hut. Before, Krishna could start the Aghori spoke, "Do you know what a Masan is?" To which Krishna answered in no. To which the Aghori spoke, "In Hindu folklore, Masan refers to a vampiric spirit which feeds off of children and exists to terrify them. Masan itself is the ghost of a child. Its shadow would cause children to slowly wither away. Masani is a spirit which hangs out around funeral pyres, attacking anyone who passes by them." Krishna had a quizzical look on his face, to which the Aghori continued further. "When I was just starting to get in the folds of Aghori

Samuday I came across the mantra to harness the power of Masan, which are pretty powerful force of nature. As an inexperienced novice I felt overconfident in mastering the force and without understanding its consequences. I was able to master one but at the cost of my fellow companions." The weight of pain and guilt in his eyes, made him look a lot older. He continued, "After that, my Guru gave me an earful for such a huge mistake and informed me, Masan will remain with me till my last breath and there is no other way. I accepted it as my destiny and dedicated my whole life learning complicated Aghori Vidyas as much as I can in hope of one day finding the answer. But alas I still had not."

"The spirit still resides with me and after night fall with my powers I am able to bind it inside the hut with me, rather than roaming the funeral ground and attaching itself with any innocent civilian. In response he torchers him all night long. I can either protect myself or bind the power. I can't do both at once, the Spirit is so powerful." With that, he was silent, his gaze fixed at some distant point on the horizon, with a little sadness creeping across his face. After what felt like an eternity, he spoke again, "Have you read, Srimad Bhagavatam?". To which Krishna replied in agreement. "Did you remember why Indra the king of gods, was in need of the Narayana Armor?". Krishna tried to jog his memory about the fight with a humungous devil but unable to recollect the exact details as he was more concerned on his pursuit of Khadag. The Aghori, understood his dilemma and started to narrate the story.

"As told in the narration given to Samrat Yudhishthira in the Maha Kavya Mahabharata, Vritra was an asura created by the artisan god Tvashtri to avenge the killing of his son by Indra, known as Triśiras or Viśvarūpa. Vritra won the battle and swallowed Indra, but the other deities forced him to vomit Indra out. The battle continued and Indra was eventually forced to flee. Vishnu and the rishis (sages) brokered a truce, with Indra swearing that he would not attack Vritra with anything made of metal, wood or stone, nor anything that was dry or wet, or during the day or the night. The Srimad Bhagavatam recognizes Vritra as a bhakta of Vishnu who was slain only due to his failure to live piously and without aggression." The Aghori continued further referring to the holy text which he pulled out from the bag hung on the wall, so that Krishna can follow what he is going elaborate. He asked him to open SB6.2. The face which jumped out of the page was enough to bring cold sweats to any Braveheart during the chilly Himalayan nights.

Image of Vritra

Once Krishna recovered from his initial shock, his eyes hovered on the texts. The Aghori continued ahead. "After King Indra insulted his spiritual master Brihaspati, the Asuras equipped themselves with weapons and declared war against the gods. As a result of their misbehaviour towards Sage Brihaspati, the gods' heads, thighs and arms and the other parts of their bodies were injured by the sharp arrows of the Asuras. The gods, headed by Indra, saw no other course than to approach Lord Brahma, with bowed heads for shelter and instructions. When Lord Brahma saw the gods coming towards him, their bodies gravely injured by the arrows of the Asuras, he pacified them with his great causeless mercy. Visvarupa, who was engaged by the demigods as their priest, instructed King Indra about the Narayana Armor, which enabled him to conquer the leaders of the Asuras. After chanting various mantras, Visvarupa began to chant the following protective prayer to Lord Narayana. ***"The Supreme Lord, who sits on the back of the bird Garuda, touching him with His lotus feet, holds eight weapons-the conch shall disc, shield sword, club, arrows, bow and ropes. May that Supreme Personality of Godhead protect me at all times with His eight arms. He is all powerful because he fully possesses the eight mystic powers."*** Next, he offered prayers to the Lord's personal expansions, to the Supreme Lord Krishna, and to the weapons of Lord Narayana. He thus taught King Indra how to take shelter of the mystic Armor."

"After Visvarupa was killed by King Indra, Visvarupa's father, Tvashta, performed ritualistic ceremonies to kill Indra by offering oblations in the sacrificial fire. Thereafter, from the southern side of the sacrificial fire came a fearful personality who looked like the destroyer of the entire creation at the end of the millennium. Like arrows released in the four directions, the Asura's body grew, day after day. Tall and blackish, he appeared like a burnt hill and was as lustrous as a bright array of clouds in the evening. The hair on the Asura's body and his beard and Mustache were the colour of melted copper, and his eyes were piercing like the midday sun. He appeared unconquerable, as if holding the three worlds on the point of his blazing trident. Dancing and shouting with a loud voice, he made the entire surface of the earth tremble as if from an earthquake. As he yawned again and again, he seemed to be trying to swallow the whole sky with his mouth, which was as deep as a cave. He seemed to be licking up all the stars in the sky with his tongue and eating the entire universe with his long, sharp teeth. Seeing this gigantic Asura, everyone, in great fear, ran here and there in all directions. That very fearful demon, who was actually the son of Tvashta, covered all the planetary systems by dint of austerity. Therefore, he was named Vritra, or one who covers everything. Vritra became the head of the asuras. He renounced his dharma duty to do good unto others and turned to violence, battling with the devas. Eventually, he gained the upper hand, and the devas were frightened of his evil might. Led by Indra, they approached Vishnu for help. He told them that Vritra could not be destroyed by ordinary means, revealing that only a weapon made from the bones of a sage could slay him. When the deities revealed their doubts about the likelihood of any ascetic donating his body, Vishnu directed them to approach the Maharishi Dadhichi. When approached by the deities, Dadhichi gladly gave up his bones for the cause of the good, stating that it would be better for his bones to help them attain victory than to rot in the ground. The devas collected the bones and Indra crafted the Vajrayudha from them. When they engaged Vritra again, the battle lasted for 360 days before Vritra breathed his last."

"The shower of various weapons and arrows released by the Asuras to kill the gods, did not reach them because the gods, acting quickly, cut the weapons into thousands of pieces in the sky. As their weapons and mantras decreased, the Asuras began showering mountain peaks, trees and stones upon the gods, but the gods were so powerful and expert that they nullified all these weapons by breaking them to pieces in the sky as before. When the Asuras, commanded by Vritrasura, saw that the soldiers of King Indra were quite well, having not been injured at all by their volleys of weapons, not even by the trees, stones and mountain peaks, the Asuras were very much afraid. Leaving aside their leader even in the very beginning of the fight, they decided to flee because all their prowess had been taken away by the enemy. When all the gods heard Vritrasura's tumultuous roar, which resembled that of a lion, they fainted and fell to the ground as if struck by thunderbolts. As the gods closed their eyes in fear. Vritrasura, taking up his trident and making the earth tremble with his great strength, trampled the demigods beneath his feet on the battlefield the way a mad elephant tramples hollow bamboo in the forest. Seeing Vritrasura's disposition, Indra, the King of heaven, became intolerant and threw at him one of his great clubs, which are extremely difficult to counteract. However, as the club flew toward him, Vritrasura easily caught it with his left hand. The powerful Vritrasura angrily struck the head of Indra's elephant with that club, making a tumultuous sound on the battlefield. Struck with the club by Vritrasura, like a mountain struck by a thunderbolt, the elephant Airavata, feeling great pain and spitting blood from its broken mouth, was pushed back fourteen yards. In great distress, the elephant fell, with Indra on its back."

Battle scene between Indra and Vritra

"After Indra cut off his two arms, Vritrasura, bleeding profusely, assumed a gigantic body which shook even the mountains and began crushing the surface of the earth with his legs. He came before Indra and swallowed him and Airavata, his carrier, just as a big python might swallow an elephant. The Narayana Armor protected King Indra, and with his thunderbolt he pierced through Vritriasura's abdomen and came out. Indra, then cut off Vritrasura's head, which was as high as the peak of a mountain. At that time, the living spark came forth from Vritrasura's body and returned home. While all the gods looked on, he entered the transcendental world to become an associate of Lord Mahadeva. Basically,

Vritra is represented in Western world as a dragon or serpent who represents drought and is known for obstructing the rivers." The Aghori took a long breath after the long narration. Krishna, was in awe listening to the vivid details of such an event of a great battle which happened eons ago. But a question still lingered in his mind. Krishna asked aloud, "Guruji why did you tell me this story? I mean what is the context? I came here searching for the divine Khadag of Mata, but there is no mention of that anywhere in the story." The mysterious smile again graced the lips of the Aghori and a twinkle in his eyes indicating he was not finished.

Chaturtha Adhyāya
Forgotten Legend

The Aghori continued, "Are you aware there is a complex network of tunnels below the ancient city of Benares?". Krishna, shook his head in denial. The Aghori further continued, "The ancient city of Benares is so old, that no-one is able to gauze the exact origin of this city". To this Krishna replied, "How is even possible. With modern methods like carbon dating, archaeological digs and other technologies which can even date back to Dinosaurs era and farther back, how is it that no one is able to find out", The Aghori replied, "There are many things in this world which Science is still unable to explain. This is one such thing. Let me give an example to make you understand better. There is a little-known place called, Maa Siddheshwari Mandir, a temple that is not far from the famed Kashi Vishwanath Temple. Normally, it stays hidden from the rush of tourists. There is a well located in its premises named as Chandrakoop. Legend has it that 'Chandra' the moon god, who is a devout follower of Mahadev created the well as a symbol of his dedication. The well means 'Chandra-Moon' and 'Koop-Well', naming it 'Chandrakoop'. Do you know why is it important?". Krishna had a look of bewilderment on his face. Taking it as a 'No', the Aghori moved forward, "After meditating with devotion for years, finally Mahadev appeared before him and blessed the well with mystical powers. It is believed to be older than Sacred Ganges herself. It is a stark reminder of how precious life is and ever-present reality of Death is. According to local lore if someone looks into the well and fails to see their reflection, it is an omen that they will meet their fate within 6 months. Now can your science explain the phenomenon?"

Krishna was bewildered and saturated with the information. He felt like a kid whose favourite ice cream was snatched from them in an instant. He was awaiting with batted breath for information he was expecting. The Aghori understanding is thoughts rallied on, "As I was saying Benares has a folk lore of massive network of underground tunnels. Saying goes that the tunnels expand till Sarnath, Gyan Vapi and other far-off places. But, no one is able to confirm the claims as the tunnels are deep under and in case anyone once in a while loses its way to the tunnels, they never get back to tell the tale. Now, according to some ancient lores when Asura Vritra was slain by Indra, his last residue took Refuge under the feet of one God who takes everyone who requests Asylum. Mahadev. His manifestation of Pashupatinath at Benares took him under his patronage. The story goes he is taking his time to rejuvenate and bidding his time till when he can be strong enough to manifest and take his revenge on Prithvi Lok and Swarga Lok." Krishna interjected abruptly, "But why Benares? Mahadev lives on Mount Kailash, right?".

As if reverberating with the last sentence the combined sound of bells and conchs started ringing all around them with the onset of evening Aarti. They both saw outside at the amber sky where a flock of birds were returning to their homes. Krishna got up and dialled Drauni with thousands of thoughts running at light speed in his mind. He went to the bank leaving Aghori at his hut where he was slowly closing the door with a drawn face. At the bank he noticed the water level has receded a lot with the mud bank showing up to fifteen meters. Good thing Drauni had a plank of wood on his boat, which he had extended on the mud bank. Krishna assumed the exposure of mud bank would be due to low tide, however there was a tingling sensation at the back of his neck. He ignored it and was lost in thoughts of what he learned today. Krishna was jerked to reality when the boat hit the mudbank at Assi Ghat. The steps laid bare as the water level has gone down. He asked Drauni, does this happen every evening? Drauni had a worried face while coiling the ropes around his elbow and shook his head in No. On the Ghats, leaving few most of them were immersed in the evening Aarti.

The divine sounds of various instruments were echoing across the banks, but there was a gloom spread across the air like a mist, which felt heavy on the soul. It was like darkness creeping across a dark room where a single candle is lit. With every flicker of the wick the darkness always threatened to take over and smother the faint light. Krishna shrugged off the feeling and went towards the Aarti. Try as much as he can, he was unable to enjoy the Maha Aarti as he did in the morning. The sounds felt suppressed, the lights from the Diyas felt like being seen through a thin screen, the divinity seems somehow diminished. Krishna, blamed his tiredness of the whole day for which he may be hallucinating. After the Aarti, he went to the same shop he had ate yesterday and noticed most of the people talking in hush tones and a look of concern on their face. Everyone looked worried, but when Krishna approached near them, they either stopped talking or moved a little further away. Not thinking much about it, he had some evening snack and packed something for dinner. By the time he reached his hotel he felt like he had walked a couple of kilometres and not only 500 meters. With drooped shoulders he headed upstairs to his room, too tired to think of anything else. He slept in to sleep while watching news on TV.

There was some news reporter in fur coat somewhere in the Himalayas. Reading the News scroll below, there was written in bold "A COMBINED TEAM OF NATIONAL AND INTERNATIONAL RESEARCHERS HAVE CONVERGED NEAR THE GANGOTRI GLACIER." Intrigued, he raised the volume to hear the discussion. The reporter was saying, in last couple of days the Glacier has started to melt alarmingly fast. The usual suspect of Global warming which was thought to be the cause, was quickly discarded as the Snow peaks around it didn't show any effect. This has caused a huge concern in both political and religious circles as it is the Source of most sacred river of India, Ganges. In the background, there were ultra-modern equipments getting off loaded from bog haul trucks. Rest of the people were busy setting up tents and other equipments on war time basis. The scientists have already started drilling for samples to test. While watching the news, he didn't know when he slipped in to sleep. The night also was not easy enough. He kept dreaming of monsters who were chasing them through narrow alleys and lanes. He kept tossing himself from one side of the bed to other. After few hours he slipped into a dreamless sleep.

Pancham Adhyāya
From Myth to Reality

Krishna

Krishna woke up with the sound of reporter on TV. Seems many other news channels have also reached as the news had become a huge sensation. There was a sense of urgency in the background with Paramilitary forces also landing along with some Major Political leaders. The news roll below read, "Suspect of foreign interference is a possibility as scientists unable to trace the cause of the Glacier melting. DEFENSE MINISTER GOING TO VISIT SHORTLY". As if matching the gloom of the news on TV, the morning outside is heavy with the fog. When Krishna looked at the clock it was around 10 AM. He was baffled as outside the window it looked like early morning. Tired from troubled sleep last night he hesitatingly woke up from the bed and went to the washroom to get freshen up. After getting freshened up he went down stairs to have some breakfast. The roads looked empty, and due to the heavy fog visibility was limited to a few meters he walked slowly and cautiously fearing being hit by vehicles. He reached his favourite place without any incident, however was disappointed to see it closed. Not only that shop but all the shops were closed as long as he can see. It was indeed a strange sight as it was late morning and the crowded streets were mostly empty. Here and there someone would appear from the fog and disappear again. Krishna was at its wits end unable to understand anything.

He decided to go to the ghats and talk with Drauni if he can find him as it would be difficult to row in this heavy fog on mighty Ganges. Reaching the Ghats, he was welcomed with a very heavy crowd which stood silent as if in a trance. Suspecting something tragic has happened on the ghats, he tried to get a glimpse what was the crowd watching. The crowd was so thick he was unable to get a view. Krishna tried to find a vantage point, but alas all was taken. There were people on the trees as well. What can be so tragic that such a massive crowd could be stupefied to a still. He again saw a shadow dart into an alley from the corner of his eye. With rising curiosity, he decided to follow the shadow, in to the alley. Throwing caution aside he ran in to the alley. He could see the shadow just at the edge of vision but never out of it. As if the shadow wanted him to follow him. Surprisingly enough he didn't feel scared following a strange person, in unknown alleys of an ancient city.

After almost more than an hour or so the Shadow at last Stopped in front of a temple. Through the dense fog and a fifty-watt bulb lighting up the name of the temple he noticed the name, "Siddheshwari Temple". Cautiously he approached the stranger prepared for any sudden movement. There was none. Krishna circled around to face the stranger. In the dim sun light, he saw the face of Drauni inside the shawl. Drauni uttered only one word, "Come". He guided Krishna inside the temple and they sat down near a well. There was palpable tension and sadness on his face.

Krishna, put forth his curiosity in words. "What happened?". With a heavy heart and voice Drauni stated, "The reason why I had come and settled in Benares, had come to reality. While I roamed the jungles at the foothills of Himalayas mad with anger and revenge coursing through my veins, I couldn't have a single peaceful moment for the Lord Shiva knows how long. At last, I reached the revered Mt. Kailash where the serene environment brought a little bit of peace to the raging storm within. After staying there for a long time, one day I had a dream asking me to come here to atone my sins." Krishna, burning with curiosity and with some doubt asked, "What sins? And how long were you in the Himalayas, as you don't seem to be more than 40-45 years old?" Drauni, had a sad smile as if remembering some devastating past. "Which one should I answer first? The time I spent in the Jungles and at the foothills of Himalayas was for centuries and was not in a correct state of mind to count days, weeks, months or years. The only think I remembered was the pain, humiliation and revenge which consumed by body and soul." Krishna, couldn't supress is doubt and blurted out, "You mean decades, instead of centuries, right?"

To which Drauni, took a deep breath and with fallen shoulders uttered in a sad tone, so low you could have missed in a normal conversation, "I really hope it was decades, my friend". Then he went silent. Krishna waited confused what he should ask and was the person deranged to have lost track of time. He was a bit afraid as well, to be sitting alone at this hour with a mentally unstable person at a secluded place. But Drauni seemed oblivious to it, lost deep in his past. After which seemed like eternity he looked towards Krishna with the same sad smile and pain in his eyes. He spoke again, "Krishna, I will go ahead and tell you my story, not because I trust you, just because even if you tell anyone, they will laugh on you or think you are high on some drugs. That's how far humanity has come from its roots and been blinded by self-proclaimed truth and version of history. Have you ever read or seen Mahabharata?". Krishna nodded in approval. Drauni continued, "Good, now do you know who are the Chiranjivis from our Sanatan history?". Krishna, had read about them during his search, so answered "Yes, they are Sage Vyasa, Mahaveer Parshuram, Bhakt Markandeya, Mahabali Hanuman, Lankesh Vibhishana, Maharaj Mahabali, Acharya Kripa, and Ashwatthama."

Drauni asked, "You had added title to every Chiranjeevi except Ashwatthama, why is that?". Krishna said, rest were blessed with immortality, however he was the only one who was cursed due to his sins." Drauni again asked, "What do you know about his sins?". Krishna, replied "After the slaughter of Pandav sons and other warriors in Pandav camp after nightfall, he returned to Duryodhana. After relaying to him the deaths of all the Panchalas and the Upapandavas, he congratulated Ashwatthama for achieving what others couldn't from his side. Hearing the news Yudhishthira fainted, and the Pandavas became inconsolable. They found him at Sage Vyasa's ashram near the bank of the Ganga. Ashwatthama, believing his time had come, invoked the Brahmastra against the Pandavas to fulfil the oath of killing them. Lord Krishna instructed Arjuna to fire his own Brahmastra as an anti-weapon against Ashwatthama to defend themselves. Sage Vyasa intervened and prevented the destructive weapons from clashing against each other. He ordered both Arjuna and Ashwatthama to take their weapons back. Arjuna, knowing how to do so, took it back. Ashwatthama, not knowing how, redirected the Brahmastra toward the womb of the pregnant Uttara in an attempt to end the lineage of the Pandavas. Lord Krishna intervened and saved Uttara's unborn child from the effects of the Brahmastra. Ashwatthama was then made to surrender the mani on his forehead and cursed by Lord Krishna that he would roam in the forests till the end of Kali yuga with blood and pus oozing out of his injuries." Satisfied with himself he looked at Drauni.

Drauni had a forlorn look on his face as if he was hurt by something he had said. He said, "History is always written by them who gain victory". Then he continued further, "What you said is right, but keep yourself at the place of that warrior whose father was killed by deception. His one friend was killed and another best friend was also injured by going against the war ethics. Their best warrior Pitamah Bhisma was also killed in an indirect fight as no one can take him down. Now think what will be his mental condition." Again, that lost look took over him lost in some past events. Krishna was confused what is the point of this discussion. There are some people who follow Ravana, Kauravas. The boatman seems to be one of them. Krishna didn't want to argue on ancient texts which will just lead to disagreement and never a conclusion. However, there was a sense of curiosity to know where this is leading.

Shat Adhyāya
Ashwatthama

After which seemed an eternity Drauni spoke, "Let me tell you the story from Ashwatthama from his point of view. I am not asking your sympathy or mercy for the warrior. I just want you to know the story which many people ignore or tend to. When Hastinapura offered Acharya Drona to teach the Kauravas, both Acharya and his son Ashwatthama became loyal to Hastinapura and fought on the side of the Kauravas in the Kurukshetra war. On the 10th day of the war, after Pitamah Bhishma fell, Acharya Drona became the supreme commander of the Kauravas army. He promised Duryodhana that he would capture Yudhishthira, but he repeatedly failed to do so. Duryodhana taunted and insulted him, which greatly angered Ashwatthama, causing a rift between Ashwatthama and Duryodhana."

On the 14th day of the war, Ashwatthama killed a division of Rakshasas, including Anjanaparvan - Son of Ghatotkacha, Grandson of Bheem, and also defeated Ghatotkacha. He also fought with Arjuna several times, trying to prevent him from reaching Jayadratha, who had killed Abhimanyu - Son of Arjun but was defeated. During the process of protecting Jayadratha, Ashwatthama, at one point in time, successfully saved Duryodhana's divine celestial armour and life by using his Sarvastra arrow and destroying the powerful Manavastra arrow launched by an angry Arjuna towards Duryodhana. Knowing it would be impossible to defeat an armed Acharya Drona and since Arjuna refused to kill his guru, Lord Krishna suggested a plan to disarm Acharya Drona by some means of contrivance. It was decided that Bheema would then proceed to kill an elephant named Ashwatthama, and then boast to Acharya Drona that he has killed his Ashwatthama. Disbelieving his claim, Acharya Drona approached Yudhishthira, knowing of Yudhishthira's firm adherence to Dharma and honesty. When Acharya Drona asked for the truth, Yudhishthira responded with 'Ashwatthama is dead, the elephant.' Adding the word elephant indistinctly so that Drona could not hear it.

Dhrishtadyumna used this opportunity to kill the grieving Acharya Drona as revenge against Acharya's killing of his father, Drupada. After learning of the deceptive way his father was killed, Ashwatthama became filled with wrath and invoked the Narayanastra against the Pandavas. Knowing that the astra ignores unarmed people, Lord Krishna instructed all the troops to abandon their chariots and disarm. After getting their soldiers to disarm the astra passed by harmlessly. The Narayanastra destroyed one Akshauhini of the Pandavas army. Seeing his Narayanastra fail to kill the Pandavas, Ashwatthama invoked the Agneyastra and launched it toward all the visible and invisible foes. The weapon soon overpowered and encompassed Arjuna with several fiery flaming arrows and created havoc within the Pandavas army. Arjuna used his Varunastra to subdue the effects of the Agniastra, but by then it completely destroyed another Akshauhini of the Pandavas army, which only Arjuna and Krishna managed to survive. Later, Ashwatthama defeated Dhrishtadyumna in direct combat but failed to kill him as Satyaki and Bheem covered his retreat, in the process engaging in a battle against Ashwatthama. Ashwatthama defeated both the warriors and made them retreat from the battlefield, as well.

Ashwatthama fired millions of arrows at a time, which resulted in the stupefaction of Arjuna himself. Ashwatthama again tried to overpower Arjuna, but at last, Arjuna defeated him by piercing his body with several arrows which made him unconscious and his charioteer took Ashwatthama away from Arjuna. King Malayadhvaja of the Pandya Kingdom, one of the mightiest warriors of the Pandavas, fought against Ashwatthama. After a long duel of archery between them, Ashwatthama rendered Malayadhvaja weapon less and got an opportunity to kill him on the spot, but he spared him temporarily for more fighting. Malayadhvaja then proceeded against Ashwatthama on an elephant and threw a powerful lance, which destroyed the latter's diadem. Ashwathama beheaded Malayadhvaja, cut his arms and also killed six soldiers of Malayadhvaja. Seeing this, all the great warriors of the Kauravas army applauded Ashwatthama for his act.

After the terrible death of Dushasana, Ashwatthama suggested Duryodhana make peace with the Pandavas, keeping in mind the welfare of Hastinapura. Later, after Duryodhana was struck down by Bheem and faced death, the last three survivors from the Kauravas side, Ashwatthama, Acharya Kripa, and Kritvarma, rushed to his side. Ashwatthama swore to bring Duryodhana revenge, and Duryodhana appointed him as the Commander-in-Chief after Shalya was slain earlier during the day. Along with Acharya Kripa and Kritavarma, Ashwatthama planned to attack the

Pandavas camp at night. When Ashwatthama reached there, he encountered Lord Shiva in a terrifying ghost form guarding the Pandavas camp. Not recognizing him, Ashwatthama fearlessly started attacking the terrifying ghost with all his powerful weapons but failed to inflict even any damage upon it. Shortly, a golden altar manifested before him and he offered himself as a sacrificial libation in exchange for passage into the camp. Lord Shiva appeared in his true form in front of Ashwatthama and offered him a divine sword. Then Lord Shiva himself entered the body of Ashwatthama, making him completely unstoppable.

After Ashwatthama entered the camp, he first kicked and awakened Dhrishtadyumna, the commander of the Pandavas army and the killer of his father. Ashwatthama strangled the half-awake ultimately choking him to death. Ashwatthama proceeded with killing the remaining warriors, including Shikhandi, Uttamaujas, Yudhamanyu, Upapandavas and many other prominent warriors of the Pandavas army. Even though many warriors tried to fight back, Ashwatthama remained unharmed due to his body being possessed by Lord Shiva. Those who tried to flee from Ashwatthama's wrath were hacked down by Acharya Kripa and Kritavarma at the camp's entrances. After that, the three warriors returned to Duryodhana. After relaying to him the deaths of all the Panchalas and the Upapandavas, he congratulated Ashwatthama for achieving what Pitamah Bhishma, Acharya Drona, and Karna could not before breathing his last breath..After that is what the whole humanity remembers as 'Curse of Ashwatthama'. I am not saying what he did is justified. However, you need to understand losing all his near and dear ones within a span of couple of weeks would have made any sane person unstable. He is not proud of what he has done and he had thousands of years to ponder upon his mistakes and anger which had given him this cursed life." He fell silent after such a long monologue.

Krishna was amazed that he had read it along with the complete Mahabharata, but had not given this part much importance. However, something stuck at the back of his mind. How Drauni can know how what Ashwatthama feels like. Then maybe, he is just guessing. As if reading his thoughts, Drauni replied, "You are thinking how I know he is repenting till now for those few moments of anger. That is because I am that unfortunate man who is cursed till the end of Manvantara". Krishna was shell shocked with this information at first, then as with every other human being doubt started creeping and his previous suspicion of a mentally ill person seemed to be true. Then also just to humour him, he asked, "Why do you think you are Ashwatthama?". Drauni smiled and said, "See I had told you at the beginning even if you tell this no one will believe you." Then started opening is head turban. Slowly a gaping hole on his forehead starting to reveal itself. It seems like someone had taken a hammer and hammered the skull till possible. Krishna was taken aback by the scene. He was wordless seeing the Myth manifesting into reality before his very eyes. And truly said by Drauni, even if he is to explain this to his family and friends, they will not believe them, leave alone anyone else

Saptam Adhyāya
Ancient History

The sunlight tried its best to penetrate the deep fog, creating a Halo in the sky. Other times it would have been a beautiful scene with a cup of coffee or tea. However, the mood and ambience near the Chandrakoop well was grave. Krishna recovering from a trance, at last gathered enough courage to speak up, "But, why are you telling me this? I don't mean to be rude, but what is the point of exposing your true identity to a nobody?". Drauni explained, "So that, what I am going to say you next should be taken seriously. The Aghori told me he had told you about Vritra and tunnels under ancient city of Benares. Do you believe it?". Krishna confused should he believe that or it is some ancient mythological folklore. However, what he had learnt few moments back has changed his perspective what is Myth and what is reality. He looked with a blank face at him. Drauni smiled understanding his conundrum.

He Continue this is no surprise that today, Humans, doesn't believe anything other than which they can put their fingers on. Anything back half a, millennia is a Story, Myth or Lore for them. The humanity has seen so much development in past century and more so in past decade that they become arrogant. They think they have achieved something which was never achieved in the history of humankind. Do you agree?". Krishna grasping it like a drowning person grasping even a twig or leaf to save themselves blurted out, "Yes, and why wouldn't we. We have harnessed nuclear power, are exploring Quantum Physics world we are able send rovers to other planets and also have sent an unmanned vehicle to Sun and outside the solar system as well. These were never heard off before and we are also able to see deep in to the space observing stars billions of years of back in time. We are able to reveal some of the mysteries of Space as well. Starting from dividing atoms to smaller units until the last thread, to exploring the vast expanse of Space, studying mega stars and mega planets, we have grown in leaps and bounds. So, after doing so much why wouldn't be Humanity proud of our achievements?". He finished his monologue in one breath and stopped to take a breather.

Drauni smiled in response and extended his water bottle to Krishna to take a drink. "So, you are saying that Air travel was invented by modern humans. Do you know Vimanas existed not only in India but across the world. Every ancient civilization has documentation of flying vehicles capable of air travel. It maybe, Mayans, Aztec, Egyptian, Sumerian, etc. Don't believe me, go ahead and Google and you can see for yourself." Krishna flipped open his phone and searched for 'Ancient Vimanas'. Lot of images popped up in the Image section. Drauni continued in the background, "The Germans, the Chinese and many others have been avid fans of India's ancient past and the vast knowledge that is so well documented in the ancient manuscripts. Lot more information may be residing in millions of still unread documents held in thousands of places of different Indian religions and sects. Some of them may be a gold mine of information that may propel India back to the position of glory it once held. Vimana is just one such stories. "

"In Sanskrit the word 'Vimana' means a part that has been measured and set aside appeared in Vedas with several meanings ranging from temple or palace to flying machine. References to these flying machines were common in ancient sacred texts, even describing their use in great wars, and able to fly/sail within and out of Prithvi as well as Water bodies. There is documentation of interstellar as well as interspatial time as well. Sacred text Rigveda mentions of "mechanical birds". Later texts around 500 BC talk of self-moving aerial car without animals. In some modern Indian languages, the word vimana means aircraft."

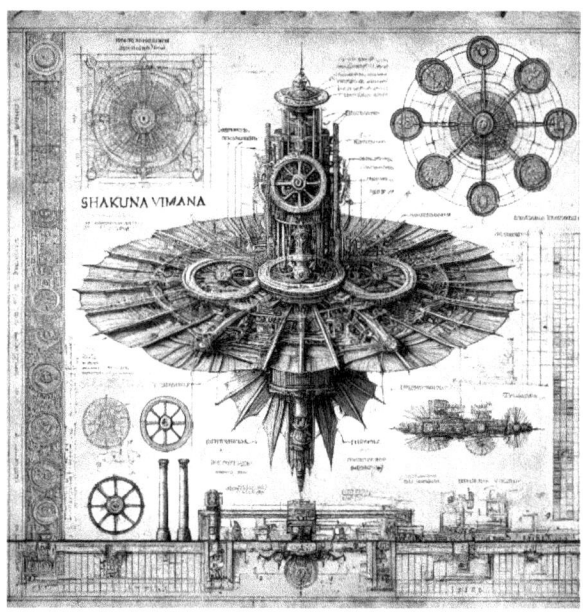

'Shakuna Vimana' might be defined as a cross between a modern plane and a rocket.

Pushpaka vimana depicted

In Sacred Ramayana, Pushpaka (the flowery Chariot) originally made by Vishwakarma for Brahma who gifted it to Kubera, the God of wealth, but was stolen, along with Lanka, by his half-brother, the demon king Ravana. It could go everywhere at will. During Mahabharata times the Vimanas were more vividly mentioned and had grown in size."

Ancient Indian flying vehicles.

Ashta Adhyāya
Monster from the Abyss

Krishna was taken aback by all that motherload of information about ancient history. Drauni, waited for a few moments to let that all settle in. After taking a gulp of water, he continued, "It's just a drop in the ocean which I told you about how advanced Humanity used to be. Another example in modern days which baffle archaeologists is how can pyramids with same architectural designs come up at same time across the world. There are many such ancient structures which baffle the modern-day academics. But that is a discussion for another day. I just wanted to make you aware Humanity today is as ignorant of their ancients as they were centuries ago. The ancient knowledge was lost somewhere in the sands of time. Now, coming to present. Do you believe the Aghori?". Krishna as if stupefied nodded his head in affirmative seeing no way to counter it. Drauni asked, "Did you remember he mentioned an ancient Asura? Vritra?". Something clicked as Krishna remembered the story and how the Asura came to be at Gyan Vapi after his demise at the hands of Lord Indra, King of Gods.

Krishna but was unable to understand how it was related to what was discussed right now. Still, he supressed his curiosity and waited patiently for Drauni to speak. After sometime he spoke, When I was roaming at the foothills of Himalayas at the advent on Kali Yuga, I was commanded by Lord Shiva to come here and wait for to fight an ancient evil. I have waited for eons to do some good which may reduce my sins a little. While staying here and discussing with Sadhus I came to know an ancient evil lies dormant in the tunnels below ancient city of Benares who used to go by the name Vritra. Even with my gem I am no match for such a powerful entity as due to advent Kali's maya my memory of warfare and weapons have degraded. Also, an entity who can take on the Devas single handedly is tough for any warrior in any Yuga unless you are an Avatar."

"When you came in search of a celestial weapon and I saw you don't want it for personal use I decided to test you. That is why I instructed the Aghori to meet you. Now, have you seen the news in the toady morning!". Krishna remembered there was some news regarding rapid depletion of Gangotri Glacier running on the TV at hotel when he woke up today. He said, "Yes, there was some news today regarding Gangotri glacier depletion. But, what of that". Drauni spoke, "From couple of decades the Sadhus have felt an uneasiness which pointed towards something disastrous towards this world. Then the Mata Ganges started to pollute unexpectedly. People thought that may be due to industries and other factors. The creepy uneasiness increased rapidly as years passed on. In past couple of months huge crowds of Sadhus, including Nagas, Aghoris across India have poured in to Benares which is doesn't bode well, as they rarely do so until something huge is happening. When I talked with them all had the same thing to say. They are unable to meditate as something dangerously evil has started stirring which has disturbed the 5 elements of nature."

"When few Siddha Sadhus went into meditation by using all their Tapa power, were able to locate the epicentre as Benares. Even most elite Sadhus and

Astrologers are unable to view the future as it appears blurry. This could only mean some major calamity is going to change the course of future. Today, all those predictions and fear has come true. The fog is due to him". Krishna was shell shocked and knew not how to react. He blurted out, "What? Do you mean to say Vritra came alive?". He jumped to his feet not sure how to react. "But how is that possible? What happened?". Drauni sighed, "As you must have known the river Ganges has medicinal properties. Seems Vritra's main intention to come to hide in Benares was to use Mata Ganges medicinal properties to regenerate his body and finish his unfinished work to destroy the Bhulok and Devlok. Due to the advent of Kali Yuga, he has rapidly regenerated and materialized sooner than expected. That is ominous not only for us but for complete world".

Krishna stood up and started to walk when Drauni held his hand to stop him. "Where are you going?", he asked. Krishna replied, "I am going to see Vritra". To which Drauni chuckled and said, "It has still not gained his full strength. But seems it had grown strong enough and impatient as well that it has come out in open and now drinking up the whole river. The speed at which it is consuming the river had led to the rapid melting of Gangotri glacier. Once it consumes enough, it will be unstoppable". Krishna interrupted, "Nothing is unstoppable, governments across the world have weapons of mass destruction which will not let a single living- organisms in its vicinity. I am sure we will be able to kill it". Drauni interrupted, "Do you think that weapons like you have today was not used against it in past? You remember the story narrated by the Aghori, right? And as I mentioned earlier during my era and Ramayana era, we used to have more sophisticated weapons which you know as Divya Astras. It was born from a Yagya and can only be killed by celestial weapons with great power. It took Indra's Vajra to take him down finally. Along with the power of Kali and its effects today it has grown more stronger than in past."

"Also, he is now underground so you can't hit him directly". Krishna interrupted in between, "Then if he is underground how you are saying all this and how you know it is Vritra?". Drauni answered, "As I said a huge number of sadhus from various sects have poured into Benares in past couple of years as they were able to meditate in the serenity and divine atmosphere of Benares. However, a couple of months back great Siddhas were also not able to meditate due to major disturbance in Pancha Bhuta or 5 Elements of Nature. A group of highly trained Siddhas went on a trip to Ashtabhuja Mata Mandir, near the Jargo Dam few kilometres South of here. It has an ancient power which helps many concentrate.They had returned back 2 weeks back with the information but were unable to predict the exact date. However, they were able to find the source of the evil – an ancient Asura Vritra. They had started their preparations as they know any evil in Kali yuga is multiple times powerful than in any other Yuga. To minimize its power and try to find a chink in the armour they have started their yagnas and chants. I who had fought uncountable monsters, warriors, devas during by lifetime, know those will not help without someone actually fighting the monster face to face."

Krishna was unable to think anything. His head felt like it contained mashed up potatoes in place of a grey matter. He couldn't discriminate between what is reality and what is fiction. The fog surrounding made it harder. It seemed to him he is dreaming a nightmare and will wake up the moment his alarm rings. He even pinched himself to be sure. Drauni saw him doing it and chuckled like a father enjoying his toddler's foolishness. At last, he was able to gather his wits and frame thoughts. He asked, "So what now?". Drauni replied, Vritra has become powerful to expand the old tunnels which ran under the Ganges. He has made a gaping hole into which all the water from the river is getting drained so he can absorb it all." "But how can he gulp so much water? Is it even possible, there is billions of gallons of water Krishna blurted out unable to wrap its head around, Drauni replied, "When Vritra was created, it serves as the personification of drought. It can gulp down rivers, water bodies to bring about drought and create mass deaths. So, it is not out of its power to drink up a complete river. It is fully capable of it. As per my guess once it gains full power and rejuvenates enough it will drink up all rivers and water bodies which are primary source of agriculture and drinking water. That will cause unimaginable scale of deaths across the world."

"Right now, he is hidden in the tunnels diverting the mighty Ganges to drink it up sufficiently to come out on earth. We have to stop it before that." Krishna spoke up,

"We? You mean you and the sadhus, right?". Drauni chuckled, "No, by WE I mean, me and you." Krishna was shocked and stood up to walk away. Drauni again held his hand to stop him. "You don't understand the gravity of the situation. Why do you think you were the only one in thousands of years who was able to locate the Khadag of 'Mata' Do you think that no one more qualified or more resourceful before you have not tried to find it before? There is a reason celestial weapons can be found only who are deserving and pure heart. You still don't understand. Let me show you what is at stake". He took his hand and pulled him towards the Ghat.

After few minutes they were at the Ghat and the crowd has thickened. Drauni with his muscular frame and towering height pushed aside the crowd and reached a barricade set up by Defence personnel. There were Military officers, Government officials, scientists and may be people from other agencies crawling at the other side of the barricade. There were massive batteries powering huge set of searchlights. The combined focus of hundreds of Searchlights pierced the massive fog and what Krishna saw made his very soul tremble. There was a massive hole in the bed of Ganges where the mighty river with a roaring sound emptied creating a dense fog. The muffled noise of rotors of helicopters flying above reached his ears. When he looked up, there were couple of helicopters flying above the hole and trying in vain to pierce the dense fog even with their powerful searchlights. It seemed to be a scene from a Stephen King's novel or movie. The fear coming from the massive hole swept over him in waves making Krishna's legs crumple below him. Drauni caught him in time and carried him to the back of the crowd. He set him supporting the wall of a temple and gave his bottle to take a couple of drinks from it.

Nava Adhyāya
The Quest

It took some time for Krishna to recover from the shock of what he said and coupled with what Drauni had explained he just wanted to roll up on the street and go to sleep forgetting anything happening around him. Then he remembered his family and suddenly he felt a warmth coursing through his blood which started repelling the gloom and fear he was feeling. After few moments he was able to gain enough strength in order to stand up. With the help of Drauni, he stood up and keeping a hand around his waist, Drauni guided him towards the Chandrakoop. Which seemed like eternity they at last reached there. Krishna took a few more gulps of water before speaking, "I felt like a tsunami of fear hit me straight in the face. I couldn't even gather my wits." Feeling embarrassed he lowered his gaze to the ground. Drauni sat beside him and patted his back to console him. He gave him some space so that Krishna can gather his thoughts. At last, he spoke up, "How can I fight such an ancient evil. It took all the Devas and Devraj Indra to take him down the first time it was done. I am a mere mortal".

Drauni smiled and said, "There were many mortals in past. One of whom who not only helped Devas in Treta Yuga but also helped Lord Krishna in Dwapara Yuga. As per sacred text Bhagavata Purana, Devas were once defeated by the Asuras. They sought refuge under King Muchukunda who is fabled to be a great warrior and a pious man. King Muchukunda fought the Asuras while he granted, devas shelter until they have a leader to fight under. When Kartikeya, son of Lord Shiva arrived to take the mantel the Devas rallied behind him and joined the fight. After their triumph, the Devas, expressed their gratitude to the king for sacrificing his privileged position on earth to travel to Svarga to help them. He was granted boon that he can sleep for his remaining years as during the fight time had flied and all his family had died on earth. When he would wake any anyone on whom his eyes fall will be burned to ashes. This boon was used by Lord Krishna to defeat Kalayavana."

"There are many mortals roaming today who are from the lineage of that King and other great humans who in past had helped Devas in their fights. They don't have any knowledge about the capability they hold, doesn't mean they are not capable of. The true bravery comes at the moment of grave dangers. And the fear radiating from Vritra always affect the person more from whom he faces greater threat. This makes me more confident that I had chosen wisely. Now, we don't have time to ponder and have to start our journey in order to at least try and stop it. Currently he is not able to get stronger as expected due to yagnas and Vedic chants continuously done by Sadhus. We have to work fast if we have any chance of defeating him." Krishna stood up to walk towards the gate, however Drauni stood near the well only. Krishna was confused.

Drauni pointed towards the well to start. Krishna with a baffled look came and stood near him. Drauni explained, "As I said Vritra is till hiding the tunnels. Also, we have to retrieve the celestial Khadag which we will need if we can get close enough. But our sole motive should be to get him on the surface. Since he had been underground for eons, the sunlight which has become more potent and the pollution in the air will impact him. The Vedic chants and power of Yagnas will also weaken him further. I hope that should give us enough leverage to defeat him. One of the many hidden openings to the tunnels is through this well. I have collected my anchor rope from my boat." Drauni tied one end to a tree and started to go down the well first. Krishna followed him. Almost three quarters down Drauni disappeared into an opening in the wall. Krishna too followed him inside the opening. The ceiling was low so they had to crouch a bit while walking. After walking for about fifty feet the ceiling rose and they were able to stand up. Drauni unbuckled his torch from his belt and switched it on. They were inside a hall-like structure which had mud chairs and a mud bed. It seemed to be a resting place for soldiers or people who used the tunnels in ancient times. Any other signs of ancient ancestors had turned in to dust with time.

Drauni spoke up with his words echoing in the chamber, "These tunnels were used by royals, their families and servants for various purposes. To pass messages, safe passage during wars or tensions and also used for illicit affairs and love birds too. There are many secrets buried within these walls. That's a discussion of another time, we have very less time to lose. Come". He darted towards a branch in the hall and Krishna followed him, darkness engulfing the hall behind them to be again waiting for a ray of light after maybe hundreds or thousands of years. Drauni spoke in hushed tone as the words were echoing, "The Aghori had told me, you mentioned him about the location of the Khadag. When I heard I exactly knew where to go" Krishna asked, "But how do you know so much about the tunnels?". Drauni replied, "When I came here, I was still ashamed of my guilt and didn't want any company. Also, I was afraid people will start asking questions and I was in no mood for question answers. Therefore, as I knew about the tunnels I searched for the opening and found this one, when one day I saved a lady who jumped in to the well to end her life. While climbing back, I saw the opening in the wall. I knew this must be an opening to the fabled tunnels of Benares."

He has to now speak loudly as the sound of raging water started drowning his voice. "I think we are closing on near the river. The tunnel opens near the river bed of Assi river but due to some mythical powers the river water doesn't enter the tunnels. You can directly walk into the bottom of the river from the tunnel". He took out a stretch of rope while they neared the mouth of the tunnel and handed one end to Krishna. "Tied that end to your waist as the water flow at the bottom of the river is very strong and the water has less visibility. So, to prevent from drifting away we need to be tied with each other. Make sure you tie it securely. We have only on torch. We both will scan the river bed for the Khadag. Anyone who finds it will give a tug to the rope so that the other can stop the search and return back to the tunnel." He tied the anchor rope to a hook in the tunnel and another end to his ankle. Once ready they both took a deep breath and jumped into the river.

Once Krishna entered the stream, he felt the full force of the river. With tons of water flowing above and the strong current he was for few moments unable to tell which was up or down. Then he got a tug on his rope and balanced himself gathering his senses. The visibility was very low and he could see the dim diffused light of the torch scanning the river bed. He used his hands to scan the river bed as much as he can. After a few minutes he started feeling breathless and tugged at the rope multiple times to let Drauni know. They returned to the tunnel by using the second rope as guide. Once inside Drauni spoke up, "I sometimes forget that humans can't stay underwater for long. I don't need to breathe regularly under the water so it's hard for me to calculate the time. Let's do one thing. You gather your breath here and I will come back once I find anything. Just keep an eye on the rope tied to the hook. Don't let it slip". Saying this he jumped back in to the river.

The time seemed to move slowly while Krishna sat at the mouth of the tunnel waiting, holding the rope in one hand. While sitting there he started to recollect the events of past few days. How, he came to know about an ancient evil who had laid dormant, bidding its time. Met with one of the Cheeranjeevi's who before today he considered as mere stories. Saw the ancient evil first time and couldn't even stand the sight of that horror. Doubt started creeping inside him. If can't stand the sight of Vritra, how will he be able to fight and kill it? He started doubting himself and was so burdened that tears started to roll down his cheeks. At that moment just like previously in the day the thoughts and pictures of his family passed his mind and a determination started building inside of him. He clutched the rope tightly to gain strength and how he will fight Vritra. In his mind he started making battle plans and strategies. He was so lost in his thoughts that he didn't notice the rope going slack and jumped in alarm when he realized Drauni standing above him.

There was a sense of urgency in his voice. "We have very little time left as I can feel Vritra growing stronger. Soon he will be strong enough. I think I have found something, let's go. Krishna while hurriedly tying the rope around his waist asked, "If you found it, why didn't you bring it with you". Drauni with grave sadness replied, "I can't as I am cursed and any divine weapon is prohibited for me to touch. Come, we don't have time to chit chat". They jumped into the river once again and swam towards the eastern side of the river. After swimming for a few yards, they could see the faint yellowish glow on the river bed. They swam towards it and Drauni, signalled Krishna to go ahead and search there. Krishna went ahead and using his hands started to search the river bed. There was hump at the bottom and he started to dig. After a few feet of digging, he touched something metallic. Leveraging on his feet he tried to pull it out. After a few jerks the Khadag (Sword) came loose, but unfortunately the sword cut through the rope binding him to Drauni. Like a straw in strong current, he was swept away the strong current in a moment. HE couldn't get his bearings and let go of his breath. He gulped loads of river water and just when he thought he will drown he was thrown out of the river.

Krishna landed on the mud and was unable to get his bearings for a few moments. Luckily, he had not let go of the Khadag. It seemed he had landed in a gorge. There was vast expense and, on both sides, very high earthen walls ran parallel till eyes could see. It seemed he was transported to a new world.

Dasha Adhyāya
Purification

It hit Krishna like an oncoming truck when he realized he was at the river bed of the Mighty Ganges. This is what had saved his life. About 30 feet above the Assi river emptied in to the bed. Now the river seems like a waterfall with the mighty Ganges dried up. The soft slit and mud is what had saved his life, otherwise the force and height he was thrown out if not kill him, would have injured him majorly. The roar of the Assi Waterfall was drowned by massive roar caused by the Ganges emptying in to the hole in the river bed. He started feeling the same fear he felt earlier that day, but the power radiating from the Khadag helped him keep his sanity. He started walking in the ankle-deep mud towards the Assi Ghat in ankle deep mud. However, he was a little disappointed as he thought the celestial weapon would be very magnificent and he couldn't put his finger on it but he expected some kind of fanfare just like in movies.

After treading through the mud laboriously for almost an hour he was able to scale the ghats. Drauni was already there with a couple of very old looking Sadhus. He had a grave look on his face and seemed to be in deep discussions with them. The moment he saw him a smile spread across his face reaching his eyes and ran towards him. Gave him a bear hug while all the eyes were on both of them. After enquiring about how come he survived and came to be he introduced him to the Sadhus. They were representatives of the various sects of Sadhus who were waiting for the Khadag. As if Drauni could read his thoughts, told him "Don't be disheartened. The full power of the Khadag has not been awakened still. It is like a candle flame now not the sun which shines. Hand over the Khadag to the sadhus who will use their siddhis and powers to awaken the celestial weapon. Once Maa threw the Khadag it went dormant and after staying for eons lying dormant it needs to be purified and awakened."

Krishna handed over the Khadag to an Aghori sadhu. He took the Khadag and touched it to his head chanting some mantra. The group of Sadhus left immediately. Drauni and Krishna followed them at a distance. Krishna explained him in detail why actually happened after he pulled out the Khadag from the river bed. They reached a open place like a field which was dotted with Yagna kunds surrounded by sadhus continuously. There was a huge Kund at the centre which remained unlit. The Group they were following moved towards this and took their respective places. The Khadag was kept on a ceremonial pedestal and the Yagna started which each Sect representative chanting in Chorus. Krishna and Drauni sat at the steps and watched them perform various ahutis of multiple elements in the Yagna Kund.

Slowly the chanting grew louder and louder and the fire took monstrous shape. The flames were almost seven eight feet high glowing strong. The more vigorous the fire became, the more the chants grew louder, the Khadag had started to glow brighter and brighter. The chanting was reaching the crescendo and loudest with the fire reaching great heights. When the final offering was offered in to the Yagna Kund, the Khadag flew on its own and floated top down on the top of the Yagna Fire. Seeing this all across the field the Sadhus stood up continuing their chanting louder and more vigorously. The Khadag seemed to simmer in the hot air with all those energies rising from 100's of Yagnas. At first Krishna thought he was imagining that the sword was absorbing the fire. Then he saw strings of fire rising from each and every Yagna fire reaching out and connecting the Khadag. Slowly the strings grew broader as the Khadag started to absorb the energy and glow brighter and brighter until it was painful to even look at.

The brightness was eye piercing but the warmth from it was soothing to the soul and mind. After consuming all the fires burnings across the field, the Khadag slowly started to descend and hovered just above the Central Yagna Kund. After a few moments the brightness dimmed to a golden glow, and the Khadag was humming with energy. Krishna was spellbound just looking at. Chants of 'Om Namah Shivaya' and 'Har Har Mahadev' Echoed across the field filing the atmosphere with divinity. The same Aghori who took the Khadag from Krishna motioned him to come forward and take the Khadag. Krishna didn't know how to approach but as if pulled by an invisible force got drawn towards the Khadag. All the Sadhus bowed their head and folded their hands in respect to the Divine Khadag. When Krishna touched the Khadag it was warm to the touch but not uncomfortable. He felt like he had immense power coursing through his veins.

Then suddenly it seemed the warmth in his veins slowly started to grow warmer and he felt like he is starting to burn from inside. He wanted to drop the Khadag, but it was like stuck to his hand and he was unable to unfurl his fist. He felt a hand touch his shoulders and something slipped on to his neck. Just as suddenly has started, the warmth started to diminish to a pleasurable warmth. When he looked at his chest there was a Ek Mukhi Rudraksha pendant hanging from his neck. Another Sadhu who was taller and older than the rest was standing beside him. He spoke with a tone resembling rocks rolling down a hill, "No mortal can control or absorb the strength of this Divine Khadag. That is why I have given this Rudraksh to you which is blessed by the power of all your Siddhis and meditation. It will help to control and contain the immense power you are holding now for some time. You have to defeat Vritra within that time or the power will burn you to ashes and until the Khadag finds another suitable candidate no one can even come near it. In which case it will be too late to save the world". They then undressed both of them and dressed them in traditional warrior attire. A saffron dhoti tied in warrior style and a piece of cloth tied from their shoulder to waist. Krishna felt light shedding his jeans, shirts and other accessories.

Krishna with the power coursing through his veins was at last ready to overcome his fear. The Sadhus then went to Drauni and handed him a Sword along with a Dhanush and Quiver with some arrows. Another Aghori came and gave him a Javelin. They explained him these weapons may not be the divine weapons he used during his battle in Mahabharata, however they have been entrusted with their Tapobal which make them far superior from any normal weapons. Drauni was surprised that they knew who he actually was. The

Aghori walked up to him and said, "Ashwatthama we knew it was you the moment you set your foot in Benares. Nothing is hidden from Yog Shakti. Do you think that you saw the women jumping in the Chandrakoop coincidently? We knew you wanted to be left alone and also some time to do self-introspection. The fabled tunnels were the only place you can do that. We planned all this so that you can have your piece of mind and when duty calls you would be ready". Ashwatthama folded his hands in respect to the great seers and now both of them armoured with celestial and powerful weapons started back towards the Ghat to take on an ancient evil.

When they neared the Ghat they could hear sound of shots being fired. Upon reaching the Ghats they saw deformed animals of all kinds emerging from the hole and engaging in fight with the forces. They looked very disgusting and horrible. It seemed each one was made with parts of multiple animals as if a kid had broken his toys and again tried to attach them not knowing which part belongs to which toy. There was a monster with the head of a chicken, body of a dog and the beak filled with sharp teeth and a snake tongue. There was another one which looked like a mix between a Bear and Goat with a long neck like Giraffe. The forces held their line while killing them with military precision, but the monsters seemed to be never ending and gradually increasing in number. Drauni looked concerned, he turned towards Krishna and spoke, "It seems we have very less time. Vritra has grown strong to summon his minions from Patal lok. Slowly he will be calling upon his fighters and then the bigger and more powerful Asuras will come who can't be stopped with bullets or small explosives. It seems Vritra has also sensed the Khadag and doing everything to stop anyone from reaching it. This is good news for us as it will be diverted in using its power to draw up his army from Patal Lok. But we must hurry".

They both started to Jog towards the Chandrakoop from where they have entered previously. Once down the tunnels Drauni again unbuckled his torch and they started towards their destination. Drauni looked conflicted, so Krishna asked him what is bothering him. Drauni spoke, "There are multiple problems we are going to face before we even reach Vritra. First it is an expert in Maya. You expect illusions and deceptions. During my prime I fought great mayavis like Ghatotkacha and many more. I was unable to pierce his illusion. They were Great Asuras but not as expert as Vritra. I don't even know what to expect. Then comes the problem of its minions who will be protecting the tunnels leading to it. Even if by any chance we pass all of them we need to face the cause of all this, a manifestation of Chaos itself. If we engage it in battle and it moves to fight with us then the waters of Mighty Ganges which it was gulping till now will have only one way that is into the tunnels. The ancient magic which doesn't let water enter into the tunnels will not be able to stand the whole might of Ganges and mostly will give away. We both will be swept away in an instant without even landing a single blow".

Krishna understood how grave the situation is. The thing for which he was most afraid now seems minor with the current problem. He looked towards Drauni waiting for an answer to the conundrum. Drauni too seemed occupied how to tackle the problems. The old warrior seemed to be showing itself in the face of this challenge. All those experience of numerous fights in life time should come handy in this situation. They kept walking in the tunnels with only the light of the torch to guide them. Drauni at last spoke, "By any luck if we are able to reach Vritra, I plan to use '*Bhaumastra*' - Bhumi's celestial weapon. The weapon could create tunnels deep into the earth. That way I can redirect the water from Ganges to not protect us. Now we can concentrate on the illusion. There is a weapon '*Mohini Astra*' – A Celestial weapon named for Mohini, the female avatar of Vishnu. It produces a mesmerising song and dispels *maya* or illusion in the vicinity. But it's a short in the dark as we don't know how strong the illusion is. Let's tackle how we fix it when the problem comes".

Ekaadasha Adhyāya
The Fight

They proceeded further in the tunnels. Suddenly they stepped in to a patch of absolute darkness where the light of the torch also didn't work. They were unable to see anything at all. Seemed they have reached the first illusion. Although they were only few inches apart their voices were very muffled. Drauni has to shout to let Krishna know to step a few feet back as he was going to summon '*Mohini Astra*'. Krishna couldn't tell up from down in that absolute darkness and stepped back a few steps waiting for the Darkness to subside. Just as suddenly the darkness had set upon them it subsided and they were able to see again. Krishna muttered a prayer to be lucky enough to have an immortal warrior by his side. They moved ahead. After going around 100 meters, they took a left turn and they saw the tunnel narrowing itself to a pin hole size in farthest corner. There was no other way to go and the only route can only be crossed by someone the size of a fly. Drauni closed his eyes to summon the '*Mohini Astra*'. Then he pointed his torch towards the point and shined the light. Infront of Krishna's astonished eyes the tunnel widened to the normal width.

Krishna was speechless as well as confused. He previously thought Drauni had used his Bow and arrow to summon the '*Mohini Astra*'. But seeing him using the torch confused him. Understanding the confusion Drauni replied. Its not always necessary to use your bow and arrow. You can summon Divya Astras from anything. I had used a blade of Grass to summon '*Brahmastra*' which was major cause of my curse. Some Astras can also be used by thoughts and don't need a physical medium. Come let's proceed, I will explain them in details later if we stay alive." They walked further deep in to the tunnels cautious of any further traps or illusions. Before the next turn Drauni motioned Krishna to stop and peeked around the bend. He turned around and spoke, "There are guards stationed in front of tunnels leading to the Vritra. I counted around 18 of them and there may be more. Stay put here while I dispose them off and come back. Don't do anything stupid!" With that he stepped past the bend and Krishna could hear shrieks and cries along with the sounds of metal on metal while a mini war waged on.

After around thirty minutes the last cry was heard and Krishna waited in the darkness for Drauni to return. Soon enough Drauni returned with saliva and blood all over his body. Without waiting any more, he motioned Krishna to follow him quietly. They both proceeded slowly, cautious of any hidden Asuras in any nook or corner. Thankfully this part of tunnel was lit by small glowing orbs floating near the ceiling of the tunnel spaced about 15 feet apart. It was not very bright but surely an upgrade from a torch. Drauni walked ahead and dispatched any minions who tried to stop their way. The tunnels were sparsely populated with comparison to what they have seen on the surface. For now, Vritra seemed to be unaware of their presence. And seemed it didn't consider any current threat through the tunnels, and why would it. The tunnels had been a long-lost secret with only a few people knowing about it and even fewer knew about the entrances which are distributed across many places.

After taking a few more turns they entered a massive hall which spanned across around 1000 feet from wall to wall. In the middle of the hall there was a huge slithering mass. If it was not moving, they would have thought it a heap of earth. Krishna could feel the power and fear radiating from the huge mass. However, it didn't impact him as it had impacted him earlier in the day. There was a hole below it and hundreds of monsters climbed on the mass to get out on to the surface. So, this was the source of from where the monsters were coming out. Now the problem is if they attack Vritra now, they have to deal with thousands of these monsters as well. Before he could even ask Drauni, he spoke, "Don't worry about the monsters. I will take care of them. You concentrate on hitting Vritra. Since it has grown huge and there is not enough space here, so the only way it can go is up which is exactly what we want". They both started their preparation and get mentally prepared for the fight.

Drauni for the first time took out his bow and took an arrow from the quiver. Seeing the confused look on Krishna's face he answered, "I am going to summon another Divya Astra, 'Twashtri' - The heavenly builder Weapon's effect when used against an army, would cause them to mistake each other for enemies and fight each other. Its effect will not last long so you have to deal as much damage as you can. The moment he starts moving I will fire the 'Bhaumastra' to create tunnels where the river water will be diverted. I will also fire arrows after that so that we both can deal as much damage as we can". After deciding their strategy, they stepped into the hall. Drauni looked once at Krishna and stepped a few feet ahead. Now filling his lungs to maximum, let out a war cry which will send a shiver down the spine of bravest of brave humans. It seemed as if like a single organism hundreds of eyes turned towards him.

Each one of the monsters stopped climbing and charged at once towards them. Drauni was calm as a sea which could only come after thousands of wars fought and won. He pulled the arrow till the maximum extent and murmured a few words. The arrow head started to glow and then he fired it towards the minor Asuras. The arrow just before reaching them as if dissolved in the air and the air seemed to shimmer. For a moment they seemed to stop in their tracks looking confused, then suddenly as if remembering something they started attaching each other. The scene was horrific to watch and a glimpse of what would happen if they are to let loose on Earth. They kept biting, tearing each other with such viciousness no animal, bird or human would ever be capable of. Krishna was looking at the scene dumbstruck, unable to wrap his head around how any organism is capable of such heinous violence. Drauni has to shout at him couple to times before he came to his senses. He then ran towards the mass at the centre of the hall trying hard to ignore the horrible scenes all around him. The power emanating from the sword gave him great speeds as he was able to reach the target within a few seconds.

From the corner of his eye, he could see Drauni loading another arrow on the bow. With no time to lose he started to attack with great fervour, inflicting hundreds of cuts within few seconds. The minor Asuras kept coming out of the hole but the moment they crawled out they started fighting between them leaving him two alone. In between an arrow would woosh and inflict damage on the mass. Sometimes, a huge fire will engulf and burn the mass, sometimes hundreds of arrows will pierce it at once. Seemed Drauni was attacking full one with all that he has. A black thick liquid started to seep from thousands of wounds on the mass. Slowly but surely, they had inflicted enough damage for the huge mass to take notice. It started to squirm and with that the number of Asuras started increasing with more big and more monstruous things pouring out of the whole It seemed the effect of the Divya Astra was slowly diminishing with the increased numbers and size of Asuras. Their fighting has diminished the vigour and they started looking confused. Krishna started to attack more vigorously on the huge mass cutting, slashing and piercing with mad fury.

At last, the huge mass started to stir and decrease in size. It seemed it started moving towards the surface. At that exact moment a huge burning arrow came with amazing speed and pierced the side of the monster and it let out an ear piercing, shriek. It started to move faster. When Krishna looked back, he saw Drauni running towards him. He took a big jump with the Javelin in his hand. The javelin pierced almost half into the side and Drauni held unto it, motioning Krishna to do the same. Krishna too pierced the Khadag till the hilt and held on to it. They moved along with the slithering mass towards the surface with great speed. The sides of the hole scratched the backs of both of them but they didn't lose the grip on their weapons. With the noise like a train coming out of the tunnel they emerged from the hole and both of them released their weapons from the mass and fell on the soft mud of the river bed. They got back to their feet immediately. Krishna felt the wounds on his back due to the walls scratching against it started healing slowly, But Drauni's back still oozed blood but he stood unaffected showing not a shred of pain or care.

As guessed by Drauni he diffused Sun rays and the pollution had drastic effect on Vritra. He was unable to maintain his huge size and had shrunk to a size they can afford to fight with. Still, it was around twenty-five feet high. The monster looked terrifying. It had the face, back and tail of a crocodile, the resembling bear hands and nails as long as swords. It let out a blood curdling scream when the arrows fired by Drauni fell from his body one by one. With eyes as red as blood filled with hatred and anger towards both of them, he let out another cry. Thousands of monsters bigger and uglier than before started pouring out of the hole. Shots started firing from behind along with blasts. Krishna turned around to see multiple battalions of various armed forces equipped with modern devastating weapons firing relentlessly on the hordes of monsters. Tanks and other mounted weapons which couldn't come on the river bed dotted both the sides of the bank had all their turrets armed towards the hole and fired nonstop. The air smelled a putrid odour of gunpowder, burnt earth, flesh and blood. The stench was unbearable but both of them were more concerned with the bigger threat in front of them. Even after so much gunfire and bombarding due to huge numbers of Asuras they have started to proceed ahead. Some of the bigger ones which were around 10-15 feet high had very thick hides rendering bullets of normal calibre useless. Smaller Asuras rallied behind them to protect themselves. Slowly the smaller monsters formed a wall in front of Vritra, to give him time to recover. This was not what Drauni and Krishna planned as once Vritra recovers enough it will be again a fight from start and may not be possible to defeat him.

Seeing no other way, they both rushed to attack the Asuras with loud war cries. They both fought vigorously hacking, piercing and cutting left and right. The divine sword cut through the waves of Asuras like butter but the waves seemed endless. On other side Drauni with a sword in one hand and Javelin in other was fighting like a mad maniac. The old bloodlust and eons of experience fighting thousands of wars has created a muscle memory unmatchable by anyone alive. It was a sight to behold, seeing he ducking here, jabbing there, slashing all in one fluid moment. The monsters who died broke into dust once they fell to the ground. Heaps of dust had collected around both the warriors which got blown when there was any blast nearby from tanks or RPGs. Meanwhile helicopters also had joined the firing high Calibre bullets and missiles. But slowly the Asuras started to push back due to their sheer numbers. The ammo of helicopter and heavy artilleries also had started to diminish. Both the warriors were also starting to get overwhelmed by the sheer absurd numbers.

Even the fabled great warrior of Mahabharata had started to get overwhelmed by the sheer numbers. Fighting on the ground seemed more difficult than fighting on a chariot. They were getting pushed back and the more time Vritra gets more difficult it will be to beat it. When it seemed the ray of hope would be doused by darkness a familiar war cry sounded behind them like the roar of an ocean. The war chant 'Har Har Mahadev' echoed so loudly it seemed to reverberate across the very fabric of Space and time. Taking down a huge Asura with slash across his torso cutting him in two pieces Krishna chanced a glimpse behind to know the source of the chant. The view he saw elated hi heart and new strength in his tired limbs. A massive sea of Sadhus including Aghori, Nagas, Shaivas, Vaishnavas, Shaktas and many he didn't even recognise were running towards them with bloodthirst in their eyes and dedication to protect their Dharma, their Heritage and most of all their Earth. The armed forces had stopped the firing standing in awe seeing lakhs of warriors without any self-preservation marching in unison to fight these terrible creatures. The massive wave of Sadhus crashed in to the Asuras like a Tsunami taking them down. This gave Krishna and Drauni some time to rest their tired limbs and make the next plan of action.

Drauni came near Krishna and shouted over the din of the battle, "I will instruct the sadhus to clear us a path straight to Vritra and will also try to pass the message to our Defence forces as well so that our army doesn't get killed in collateral. He disappeared in the crowd while Krishna with renewed Vighor started his fight again.

After some time, a strong hand pulled him out of the frenzy and shouted in his ear, "Message delivered, let's go". They then saw a path being cleared in the north eastern direction from where they were standing and at the end Krishna could see Vritra engaged in intense fight with the same Sadhus who performed the Yagna for the sword. The group seemed like a pride of Lions trying to take down an Elephant. They both rushed forward with amazing speed to join the battle. In an instant they were fighting shoulder to shoulder with them. Krishna was oblivious to his surroundings with blood-coloured eyes, his only target the monster in front of him. It seemed to buckle under the combined effect and slowly retreating back. Then the moment of strike presented itself when Drauni pierced his javelin behind the knee of Vritra bringing him down to a kneeling position. A sadhu also went down on his knee and bent forward providing a launching pad for Krishna to attack. Krishna took a short run and leveraging on the back of Sadhu jumped high in the air and with one clean swipe separated the head of Vritra from its body. For a few seconds the body stayed kneeled and fell with a deep thud on the river bed.

The moment he was destroyed the rest Asuras turned their heads towards them in unison and like a single organism they all proceeded to attack Krishna. Another miracle happened at that instant, tendrils rose from ground to bind the feet of Asuras and started pulling them below. The howls and shrieks were ear piercing and terrible. At last, every last one of them was pulled below leaving a field of dead bodies strewn across the river bed, slowly a stream of blood had formed from thousands of dead bodies of Sadhus. Now since the battle was over, rest of the sadhus started picking their fallen companions and carried them back to Assi Ghat. With the war adrenalin subsiding and tiredness setting in Krishna and Drauni also helped in picking the bodies of unknown heroes who selflessly gave their life knowing history will never utter their name or identity. It will be slowly forgotten in the sands of time. Once they reached the Assi Ghat, both of them sat down with a hot cup of masala tea. Drauni had numerous wounds on his bodies, but still he refused any treatment. They both sat there silently watching the Defence forces set explosives in the hole to close its face so that the river may start flowing its normal course. Following loud sirens, a series of explosions took place which sent a tremor beneath their feet, the hole fell on to itself and once it closed the mighty Ganges started came gushing forward washing the blood on the riverbed. It seemed Maa Ganga had accepted their sacrifice and granted them Moksha.

Slowly the sun started to set throwing a golden glow across the atmosphere. The temples and ghats were silent today mourning the deaths of Shiv ganas. Out of the elven sadhus who they met in the morning five had fallen in the war. The rest six had come to invite them to pay their last respects to their fallen heroes. With heavy heart and tired limbs, they went to the dormitories to take a bath wiping the blood and gore from their body. Once they got freshened up, they wore a white Dhoti and a white cloth across the torso. Then they took a public transport to Manikarnika Ghat where the last rites were to be held. The fallen heroes were laid on pyres on a bed of flowers with due respect. There were gloomy faces all around representing the great loss this has been. AS the sun started to set the pyres were lit with chants reverberating across the mighty Ganges which has regained its flow. The smoke arising from thousands of pyres lit the night sky and the smoke rising from them gave the full moon which had risen above the horizon a deep red hue. It was as if the whole world was mourning the loss of these fallen heroes. They stayed there till the pyres were burnt to ashes which was almost near to midnight. The Aghoris collected the ashes amid the continuous chanting and dispersed them in the holy Ganges. Krishna and Drauni returned back after that with the Sadhus to their tent where they had a simple meal. Sleep was nowhere near after what happened during previous day. No one was in a mood to speak and all of them stayed silent mourning the loss. Drauni slowly walked up to Krishna and handed over a Rudraksha bead which Krishna recognized being worn by the Aghori he had met first when he came to Benares. Couple of tears trickled down his cheek mourning the loss which somehow felt personal to him.

Benares

Antim
A New Beginning

Benares

Krishna, woke up to the sound of chants not knowing when he had fallen asleep last night. We woke up and saw the sadhus busy with their prayers and yagnas. The fog had subsided with warm sunlight spread across the whole world. It was exactly opposite of how the atmosphere was yesterday. Krishna woke up and went to get freshened up. After that he had some light breakfast served by a sadhu and went in search of Drauni. After enquiring around he got to know Drauni has left early in the morning. Krishna started towards the Assi Ghat with the Khadag slinging in a scabbard across his back. Someone has heavily wrapped it with cloth which looked like a bundle of cloth without any sign of what it contained. He reached Assi Ghat after around fifteen minutes by public transport. There he went towards the boats tied on the banks. There he found Drauni sitting on his boat sipping a cup of warm milk. The numerous wounds on his body have stopped bleeding but by the look of them didn't seem he had applied any medicines on them.

He approached and sat beside him on the boat. Seeing him Drauni signalled the boy working in the tea stall to get a tea for Krishna. Krishna took the hot tea and thanked the boy. Taking sip, he asked, "So what now?". Drauni chuckled and spoke, "What now?". Krishna replied, "I mean what should I do now? What will I do with the Khadag? What is the next plan of action?". Drauni laughed out aloud. He replied, "I am not some seer to tell you the future. For now, the evil has subsided but not finished. The impact of Kali has been increasing in past century and its impact can be seen all around.

Since the Divine Khadag had chosen you for this quest, it seems you have a greater role to play in this Celestial play. When the time comes you will know what to do. Till then the Khadag is your responsibility to keep safe and not let it fall in wrong hands which can cause unimaginable damage". Krishna calmly sat there sipping his team. After getting up to leave, he turned and asked, "So when will we meet again?". Drauni replied, "My identity here has been exposed and no more feasible for me to stay here. I will move out from here in the middle of the night. If our paths are destined to cross in future we will surely meet, if not then it means we are not destined to meet". Saying this he folded his hands towards the Pashupatinath Temple. Krishna realizing the conversation has concluded folded his hands and bowed his head in respect towards Drauni and started walking back towards his hotel too many questions running through his mind. Then deciding there is no point in thinking ahead of time he folded his hands towards the Pashupatinath Temple muttering 'Om Namah Shivaya' and requesting blessings of Lord Shiva and be his guide when times comes.

"Om Namah Shivaya

www.ingramcontent.com/pod-product-compliance
Lightning Source LLC
LaVergne TN
LVHW061556070526
838199LV00077B/7072